The Learning
Garden
School

Best Friends

OLD BEAR TALES
Best Friends
JANE HISSEY

Philomel Books
New York

In memory of my grandmother Julie Smith
and her ninety years of storytelling.

Copyright © 1988 by Jane Hissey.
First published in the United States of America in 1989
by Philomel Books, a division of The Putnam & Grosset Group,
200 Madison Avenue, New York, NY 10016. First published in 1988
by Hutchinson Children's Books, Ltd., London.
Printed and bound in Italy by New Interlitho Spa, Milan.
Book design by Polly Dawes and Golda Laurens.

Library of Congress Cataloging-in-Publication Data
Hissey, Jane. Best friends.
Summary: The further adventures of the playroom
toys, as they throw a birthday party, bake fruit
pies, and narrowly escape being sent to the garage sale.
[1. Toys—Fiction] I. Title. PZ7.H627Be 1988 [E] 88-19576
ISBN 0-399-21674-X
First impression

CONTENTS

BILLY BEAR AND THE PARTY OF SURPRISES

The toys all knew it was Billy Bear's birthday. He'd been telling them for weeks, to give them plenty of warning. Then, on the day, they found a huge notice written on the blackboard in the middle of the room. It said: YOU ARE ALL INVITED TO A PARTY OF SURPRISES – COME AS YOU ARE OR COME IN DISGUISES. The notice also told them that the party was to be that afternoon at the far end of the playroom. Everyone thought a party of surprises sounded very exciting. Billy thought that it was a pity he knew what all the surprises were. He had to, because he'd planned them. But it wouldn't really matter, because everyone was bound to bring him a birthday present and, "Presents are the best surprises," he said to himself.

All morning, he worked very hard preparing his

surprise party. He made jello with whole fruits hidden in the middle. He made some egg, some cheese, and some banana sandwiches, and he made little paper flag-shaped labels to tell people which was which. Then he swapped the flags round. Now the cheese ones were labelled "banana," and the egg sandwiches said "cheese." "That will surprise the others," he said. He also made a pretend cake by painting a shoe box to look like one, but he made a real cake, too, so that the toys wouldn't be too disappointed. He made a special banana milkshake for his friends to drink, but he colored it pink so that people would expect it to taste of strawberries! When he had put holes in some of the squeaky party blowers, so that they didn't quite squeak, and stuck a few paper hats together so you couldn't get your head into them, he decided that, at last, he was ready.

But, as a final touch, he hid all the food and drink around the room. "It will surprise everyone to see no food at a party," he said. "I'll let them discover it."

The time of the party came at last and everyone marched down to the far end of the playroom. As each toy arrived, Billy was handed a birthday card in an envelope with "Billy Bear" written on the front. "Thank you very much," said Billy, putting them on the table. "I'll open the cards after . . ." He was going to say, ". . .after I've opened my presents," but he stopped himself, because he suddenly realized that not one of the toys had brought him a present. Oh dear, what a disappointment. A party without presents.

Billy tried to hide his feelings, but just couldn't enjoy things in quite the same way anymore. He didn't say anything; after all you don't *have* to give people presents on their birthday. Perhaps it was silly of him to expect to be given things. He decided to make a special effort. "Come on, everyone," he said, "I'll open my cards at the end of the party. Let's all enjoy ourselves."

The toys were ready for that. They had looked forward all day to the party. Soon they were playing games and dancing. After a little while,

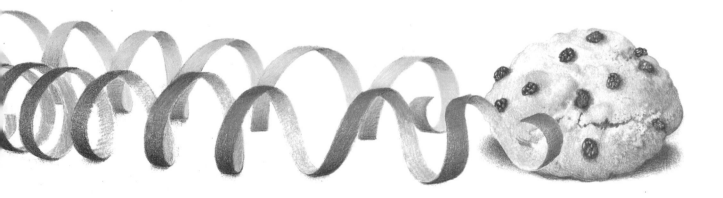

someone came across a plate of food, and then everyone began a food hunt. It was great fun. Every time they found some food, they put it on the table, and soon the table was full of the delicious party food and Billy said that it was time to eat. And then the real fun began!

The food all looked lovely, but it wasn't long before the toys were discovering Billy's little tricks and surprises. When anyone asked for a sausage roll, Billy rolled a sausage across their plate and laughed. When anyone wanted a rock bun, they found themselves with a real rock with raisins stuck to it, and painted to look like a bun. They discovered what was in the surprise sandwiches, usually only by eating them, and they thought the milk shake most peculiar, till they realized that, too, was a trick.

But there were nice surprises, too. Billy had invited a magician to come along and do some magic for the toys. His surprises were very clever.

He made bunches of flowers pop out of magic boxes, and handkerchiefs appear from nowhere. At one point, he even made one of Rabbit's friends pop up out of a hat. The toys were delighted; Billy enjoyed it, too. But it didn't quite take his mind off the thought that he hadn't had a single birthday present that day.

At last, the end of the party was drawing near; the food was all gone, except the rock buns, and the toys had played as many games with surprise endings as they could think of. Billy wasn't looking quite as happy as he should have been and all the toys knew why.

"Why don't you open your cards, now," said Old Bear, at last.

"Yes, I should do, shouldn't I," said Billy. He returned to the heap of cards on the table and carefully tore open the envelope of the first one. Out fell a birthday card that said, To Billy, with love from Rabbit.

"Thank you, Rabbit," said Billy Bear.

"There's something else," said Rabbit, "look in the envelope."

Billy peeped inside and saw a piece of paper. He drew it out and read what it said, This piece of paper entitles you to one carrot and raisin cake to be baked by me, Rabbit, on the day of your choice.

"Oh, Rabbit," said Billy, "what a lovely idea! I shall look forward to that. Will you make it when my friends come to stay next week?"

"Of course," said Rabbit. "It's your present. You can have it whenever you like."

"Thank you very much," said Billy, "it's a wonderful present."

Billy returned to his cards and opened the next one. It was from Old Bear and there was a piece of paper in that one, too. It said that Old Bear would pack Billy a picnic on the first sunny day of the summer. Billy was thrilled. He opened one card after another and, in each, there was a paper promise. Bramwell Brown promised to pick Billy a big bunch of flowers whenever he wanted one; Sailor said he'd teach him to dance the sailors' hornpipe whenever he needed cheering up; Little Bear said he'd make him a pair of trousers like his own; and Duck said that he would make him a nest whenever he wanted somewhere cosy to sleep.

There were lots more promises from all the toys. Billy was soon promised anything he could have wished for.

"Oh, thank you everyone," said Billy. "This has been the best surprise of the day. They're lovely birthday presents and they will last me all year; right up until the next birthday. But now I'm so tired that, Duck, do you think I could have your birthday present tonight? I would just love to curl up in a nice cosy nest and dream about all today's surprises."

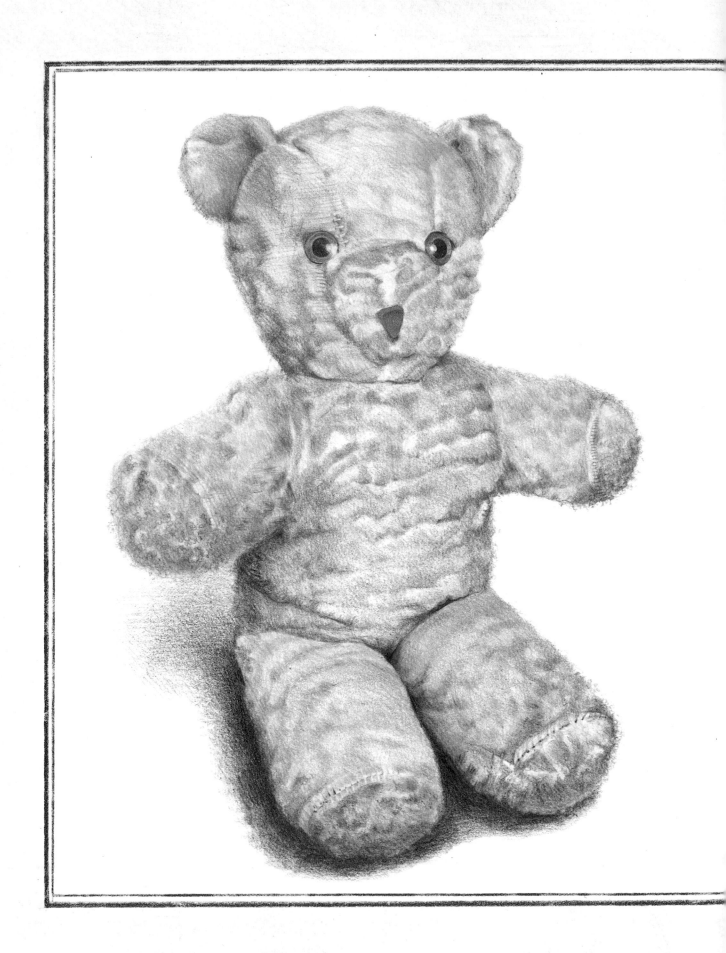

TEDDY NO-NOSE AND THE BLACK BUTTON

Teddy No-nose hadn't actually had a nose for years. He'd lost it when he was a fairly new bear and he'd managed perfectly well without one. There weren't many things he actually had to smell, and the other toys were so used to seeing him without a nose that they hardly teased him at all. In fact, some of the newer toys thought that Teddy No-nose had *never* had a nose.

One day, however, Teddy No-nose was watching some of the other toys being packed into a basket. They were going out for the day with the children, and he suddenly realized something: people always played with him at home, as much as with the other toys, but he couldn't remember ever being taken out for the day or away on vacation.

"It must be because of my nose," he said to himself. "They're too ashamed of me to take me out in case their friends laugh at me. Perhaps it's time I tried to get a new nose. But where do I find one?"

Teddy No-nose went off in search of Old Bear and asked him where he could get a new nose.

"That's easy," said Old Bear. "Take some money from your piggy bank and go to the Teddy Bear Repair Shop. They sell noses there and you'll be able to choose any nose you like."

Teddy No-nose was quite excited at the idea of choosing a new nose, until he realized that he had no money in his piggy bank. The last time he'd looked, there had just been a button in there. "Well," he said, "I shall just have to earn some money to buy a nose."

He went off straight away to ask all the toys whether they needed any jobs done. Within a few minutes, he was busy tidying up the dollhouse.

"We'll give you five cents when you've done it," said the dollhouse dolls. Teddy No-nose worked very hard and soon the little house was spotless. The floors and walls were gleaming and the furniture was all in place. "That's lovely," said the dollhouse dolls. "You've worked very hard and here's your nickel."

With the precious money in his paw, Teddy No-nose began his next job. Duck had said he would pay him five cents too, if Teddy would help him find a missing piece of jigsaw puzzle that he'd been looking for for days. Teddy No-nose searched everywhere, lifting things that were too heavy for Duck to lift, and suddenly, there, under a very big book, was the missing piece of jigsaw.

"Wonderful," said Duck, giving Teddy No-nose five cents. "Now you've got two nickels; that's ten cents altogether. I should think you could buy a new nose for ten cents."

Teddy No-nose thanked him very much and set off with his ten cents. But he only got as far as the stairs. With one coin in each paw, he had nothing to hold on with and was trying to go down the stairs just a bit too fast. He slipped, grabbed at the stair carpet, and dropped both the coins. Helplessly, he watched as they bounced down the stairs and disappeared between the cracks in the floor boards. "Oh no!" he cried, and sat down on the stairs with his head on his paws. "Now I'll never have a new nose."

"Why not?" said a voice very near him.

Looking up, he saw Monkey standing beside him. "Well, I was going to buy a nose," explained Teddy No-nose, "and I earned ten cents by working very hard, but now I've dropped it, and all I've got in my piggy bank is a button."

"Well, what's wrong with a button?" asked Monkey.

"There's nothing *wrong* with a button," said Teddy No-nose, "but it won't buy me a new nose, will it?"

"No," said Monkey, "but what color is it?"

"I can't remember," said Teddy No-nose. "I'll have to look."

Fetching his piggy bank, he undid the little cork at the bottom. Out dropped a shiny, round, black button. "What does the button remind you of?" said Monkey.

Teddy No-nose stared at the button and then he stared at Monkey. And then he realized that Monkey's nose and eyes were all made from buttons. "Of course," he said, picking up the button. "It looks like a nose."

"That's right," said Monkey. "You don't need to buy a nose because you've already got one; a button nose."

Teddy No-nose was very

excited and could hardly stand still long enough for Monkey to sew on his new button nose. It looked very smart – better than any store-bought one.

The children still didn't take him out, though. "It wasn't because of your nose," they explained. "You're just too big to fit in the basket."

But he didn't mind staying at home now, because he had a new friend, a friend with a button nose just like his.

And Monkey and Teddy No-nose spend many hours sitting together, trying to think of a name for a teddy who used to have no nose, but who now has a button. They haven't thought of one yet; I wonder whether they ever will.

THE BEDTIME
PONY

He doesn't do much in the daytime
And I can't take him outside,
Though he's a sort of pony
He's too small for me to ride;
His stuffing's rather lumpy
In his hooves and in his head,
But he's always waiting for me
When I snuggle up in bed.

He's not the sort of pony
Who can walk or pull a cart,
And no one dares to wash him
Just in case he falls apart;
His coat is rather faded
(All the pink bits should be red)
But he's always there beside me
When I'm sleeping in my bed.

DUNCAN BARKER AND THE TARTAN BLANKET

The toys were all a little worried when Duncan Barker came to live with them. The first thing he did was to chase Rabbit round and round the room. "I always chased rabbits in Scotland," he explained.

"I'm afraid I can't live here with that new dog," puffed Rabbit, out of breath from running. "I shall never have any peace."

"Don't worry, Rabbit," said Snowy the old white bear. "This morning he tried to get me to wear a kilt, but I expect he'll settle down soon."

But Duncan Barker didn't settle down. The next day he upset the dollhouse dolls by cooking porridge on their stove and not washing up the saucepan. "I always cook porridge for breakfast," he explained.

"We can't live with that new dog," said the dollhouse dolls, "we'll never have any clean saucepans."

"It's all right, he's just getting used to things,

I expect," said Snowy.

But things got worse. The following morning the toys were awakened to a dreadful, squeaking, whining noise. It was Duncan Barker, of course. He'd tried to make bagpipes out of a hot-water bottle and it hadn't worked very well. "I always play the bagpipes first thing in the morning," he explained.

"Oh no," groaned the other toys.

Well, a few days after that, there was an enormous commotion at bedtime. "Ow!" yelled Bramwell Brown. "There's something prickly down my bed!"

"Ooh!" quacked Duck. "It's got me too."

"Duncan Barker," shouted Snowy, "what have you done this time?"

"Oh," said Duncan, "I think you've found my

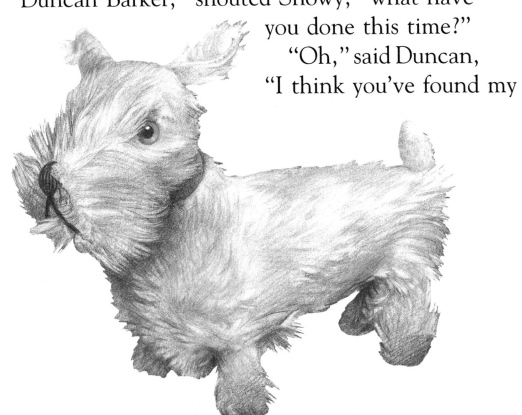

thistle collection. I always collect thistles."

"Thistles!" chorused the other toys. "Why thistles?"

"Because thistles remind me of my real home," said Duncan Barker.

"And where is your real home?" asked Snowy.

"In Scotland, of course," replied Duncan Barker.

"Well, I wish you could go back there," said Bramwell Brown, picking prickles out of his paws.

"So do I," said Duncan. And, miserably, he left the room to practice his bagpipes in the bathroom.

"Bramwell Brown, that wasn't a very kind thing to say," said Snowy. "If Duncan is missing his home, then we must make him feel at home here. If he were happier, then he probably wouldn't be so much trouble. Let's look for things that will make him feel more at home."

While Duncan Barker was out of the room, the toys rushed about getting things ready for his return. They found a lovely tartan blanket in the blanket box and put it in a cosy corner of the playroom. Then they put Duncan's thistle collection with it and a special bowl for him to have his porridge in. Bramwell Brown,

who was good at painting, painted a lovely picture of mountains and valleys and pinned it up near the tartan blanket. "There," he said, "I'm sure Duncan will like that."

And of course, he did. "Oh it's just like home," he barked, running round and round the tartan blanket. "Everyone has tartan blankets in Scotland, and what a lovely porridge bowl. Can I make you all a nice bowl of porridge?"

"Thank you very much," said Snowy, "we'd like that."

And while Duncan made them all some porridge, Snowy talked to him about Scotland.

Duncan Barker felt quite at home after that. He went to Scotland sometimes for his vacations, but the rest of the time, he lived in the little Scottish corner of the playroom and was almost no trouble at all. He never quite mastered the hot-water bottle bagpipes, though, however hard he tried.

THE GARAGE SALE

Little Bear burst into the playroom in a terrible fluster. He upset a jar of marbles and tripped over a jigsaw that had taken Rabbit all morning to do. "Quick, everyone!" he called, rolling across the room on the marbles. "It's an emergency!"

"What is it, Little Bear?" asked Rabbit, crossly. "What on earth's happened?"

Little Bear led Rabbit out into the garden and there, pinned to a tree, was the terrible sign. It said: GARAGE SALE ON SATURDAY. CLOTHES, FURNITURE, TOYS WANTED.

"Oh, no," groaned Rabbit, "not again. We'll all be sorted out, and put up for sale. Quick, let's get back and warn the others. Old Bear's ear has nearly fallen off and Bramwell's got a loose eye."

They rushed back and warned the other toys and, within five minutes, there was a line forming at Sarah Elizabeth's cupboard. Now Sarah Elizabeth was a very kind little bear; she was always mending the other toys and making new clothes for them. But today, she looked at the line of toys waiting for repairs or new clothes, and she knew she couldn't cope. "No," she said, "it's no good, I can't possibly do all this sewing and there's only one answer. If you are to be looking your best by Saturday, I shall have to teach you all to sew so you can do your own repairs and make yourselves new clothes."

So Sarah Elizabeth made her own little sign. It said: SEWING LESSONS FOR EVERYONE THIS AFTERNOON – MATERIALS PROVIDED – SMARTEN UP OR YOU MAY BE SENT TO THE GARAGE SALE.

By the time Sarah Elizabeth had had her lunch, all the toys were gathered, eagerly awaiting their sewing lesson.

"Oh do show us how to sew. We don't want to be given to the garage sale," said Sylvester Bear. "My trousers are full of holes. I must have a new pair."

Sarah Elizabeth emptied out a heap of materials from her rag bag and gave each toy a needle and some thread. All afternoon, she showed them how to make jackets and trousers, bow ties and ribbons. She showed them how to darn noses and mend ears, how to sew on eyes and patch threadbare paws. The toys all listened carefully and worked

very hard. None of them wanted to go to the garage sale. "Well done," said Sarah Elizabeth, when Bramwell mended Old Bear's ear and Old Bear repaired Bramwell's eye. The two bears looked very pleased.

Sylvester needed trousers and, sorting through the rag bag, he found some tartan material that he decided would really suit him. Sarah Elizabeth helped him to cut out the shapes he needed and then he sewed them together himself. His trousers looked wonderful. Then everyone wanted trousers.

Rabbit and his cousin Reggie made themselves whole sets of clothes. "Nobody will give us to a garage sale," said Rabbit. "We look like new toys." It was true, they all looked brand new. Their ears were fixed on firmly, their paws didn't have any holes and their eyes weren't hanging on by a thread.

Sarah Elizabeth was very pleased with everyone. "I won't have to sew for you any more," she said. "You are all really good at it. Now I can have a vacation whenever I want one."

The next day, the day of the garage sale, the whole family came into the playroom to look for toys that could be given away. "I'm sure there are some that have noses or ears missing," said the children's mother. "Let's have a look."

They walked round the room and found a row of toys sitting there, smart, clean, well dressed and without a single wobbly nose or ear between them.

"It does seem strange," said the children's mother a few minutes later as she walked out of the room, "I never realized what good condition all the toys were in. I thought I'd find lots to give away to the garage sale, but all I could find were these," and she held up a bag of marbles and a jigsaw puzzle. "Perhaps we'll find some broken toys for the next garage sale," she said.

But now that all the toys could sew they never allowed themselves to get threadbare again. And as a very special thank you to Sarah Elizabeth, they all made her a beautiful new dress. "We want you to have this," they said, "because you saved us from being given away, and now we never

need to worry about notices pinned to trees, again."

And, just for fun, they played garage sale themselves, using all the old threadbare clothes as things to sell. "We won't have toys at our garage sale," they said. "You can never be sure they are going to good homes and we wouldn't want to worry them."

FREDDIE AND THE BLACKBERRIES

I t was a muddy, misty autumn day and Freddie the teddy decided it was just the day for a walk. He went to the cupboard to fetch his boots and there he found something which didn't belong to anyone in his house. It was an umbrella, but it wasn't just any umbrella, it was a bright red one with a teddy-bear handle carved out of wood. "Oh dear," said Freddie, "I know who that belongs to and I shall have to return it straight away."

The umbrella belonged to a teddy bear friend of Freddie's, Alexander Bear, who lived just across the field with another family of children. He'd been to visit Freddie the day before and had forgotten to take the umbrella home.

"Well, it makes a good excuse for a walk," said Freddie, putting on his boots and picking up the umbrella. "I shall go and see Alexander straight away."

Singing happily to himself, Freddie set off down the garden and through the hedge into the field. The field itself was very muddy and Freddie found that the only way to go was round the edge where the ground had not been plowed up by the tractor. Then he noticed something he'd forgotten all about since last year. Blackberries! Big, bright, black, juicy blackberries, hanging there, just waiting to be picked. Oh, I'm sure Alexander Bear would love some of those, thought Freddie. We could have them for tea! And he started to pick pawfuls of the juicy fruit. Soon, he couldn't hold any more.

"I really need something to put them in," he said, "but what can I use? I didn't think to bring a basket with me." And then he remembered the umbrella – Alexander's umbrella. "Of course," he said, "if I open up the umbrella and hold it upside down, I can fill it with blackberries."

And so he did. He picked and picked until the umbrella was full of the best and most delicious blackberries. Then, as it looked as though it might rain soon, he hurried off along the path toward Alexander's house.

The path was muddy, but Freddie had his boots on so his feet stayed dry. When he was nearly there, the grey clouds could hold on to the rain no longer, and big drops started to patter on to Freddie's head. That's all right, thought Freddie, I've got Alexander's umbrella to keep me dry.

Jane Hissey

And, without thinking, he lifted the umbrella up above his head.

For a moment, Freddie thought that it was raining blackberries, and then he realized his dreadful mistake. When he'd lifted up the umbrella, all the lovely berries had fallen out, bounced off his head, and landed on the path. Miserably, Freddie watched as they sank into the thick, brown mud and disappeared forever. "Oh no!" he said out loud. "Now we won't be having blackberries for tea after all."

Sadly, he walked on to Alexander's house and knocked on the door. The little bear was delighted to see him and was really pleased to have his umbrella back. "Thank you, Freddie," he said, "that was so kind of you. Now come and see what I've been doing."

And he led his friend through to the kitchen. A wonderful smell met Freddie's nose as he walked into the room. There, amidst the pots and pans, was a row of gleaming jars of jam. "It's blackberry and apple," said Alexander proudly. "There's a jar for you and some for our tea and there are enough blackberries and apples left for us to make a pie."

Freddie laughed, and told Alexander all about his blackberry picking, and how they'd all fallen out of the umbrella. "Perhaps it's just as well I

didn't bring you any," he said, smiling. "I don't think you could have managed more. You'd have run out of jam jars!"

And the two friends sat down to enjoy their tea.

PETER AND THE PUMPKIN BEAR

Peter Bear sat in his usual place on the windowsill, looking out at the people walking by. Everyone knew Peter was there and every now and then someone would come close to the window and talk to him through the glass. Peter loved all the attention. He would stay there for most of the day and was never lonely for a minute.

Today was a special day. It was the last day in October, Hallowe'en, and lots of people stopped to tell Peter about their exciting plans for parties that night. Before long Peter saw the two children who lived with him coming home from school. They were each carrying a fat, bright, orange pumpkin. Peter thought these might be to eat, but the children had other ideas.

"Look Peter!" they cried, rushing into the house. "We're going to make faces with these and put candles inside."

While Peter watched with excitement, they carefully cut off the top of one of the pumpkins, then they began to dig out the middle with a spoon. That looks fun, thought Peter. But when the children cut a face for their pumpkin Peter changed his mind. He could hardly bear to look – the horrible, cross, monster face had staring eyes and gappy teeth in a wicked sort of grin. The children were delighted, but Peter put his paws over his eyes. With the help of their parents, the children put a candle inside the pumpkin head and lit it. Straight away the pumpkin face shone with a fiery, red glow. It looked even more frightening now and seemed to stare at Peter. When the children put it on the windowsill it glared out at the people walking by and nobody dared to come near the window.

When everyone had left the room, Peter peeped out from behind his paws. "What can I do?" he said. "With that thing there frightening everyone, nobody will come over to talk to me." He crept over to blow out the candle, but thought the children would be cross with him if he did that. And then he saw the other, unused pumpkin and an idea came to him. Using the knife and spoon the children had used, he cut the top off the spare pumpkin and hollowed out the middle. Then he began to cut a face in his pumpkin, but his pumpkin face was a happy, friendly face. In fact it was the face of a smiling teddy bear. Peter carried

the finished pumpkin to the windowsill and put it down carefully beside the monster face. Then, as he knew he shouldn't use a candle in case he burnt his paws, he fetched a torch to put inside his pumpkin bear. Straight away it smiled out with a warm, orange glow and the people walking by were so surprised to see a friendly bear face that they came over to take a closer look. All Peter's friends arrived to talk to him about his pumpkin and they took no notice of the monster face at all.

In fact so many people liked Peter's idea that they all made pumpkin bears too. And it turned out to be the most unfrightening Hallowe'en anyone had ever known.

THE CHRISTMAS FANCY DRESS PARTY

The Christmas holiday seemed to be a time for the new toys. All the old ones found themselves sitting upstairs with nobody to play with. "It's not very exciting, is it?" said Mo, the mohair bear, as he paced up and down the playroom.

"Well, we could do something exciting," said Old Bear. "Let's have a fancy dress competition, a Christmas one."

"That's a good idea," said Rosie and Fluff, two very small bears. "We know what we could dress up as." Whispering and laughing, they rushed off into a corner to plan their costumes.

Soon all the toys were busy finding, making, or trying on their fancy dress costumes. They were all very excited. "I'm going to dress up as a king," said Mo. "I can just imagine myself in a beautiful crown."

"Where will you get a crown?" asked Little Bear.

"I shall pull a cracker," said Mo. "They always have paper crowns inside."

Old Bear and Little Bear settled themselves down in a chair to judge the competition. Rosie and Fluff had left the room to fetch something. "They said they wouldn't be long," said Old Bear. "When they come back we'll start the judging." Looking round the room he didn't recognize any of his friends any more, they were all in disguise. "They do look like good costumes," he said. "It's going to be very hard to judge the best."

Everyone was eager to get started and still Rosie and Fluff weren't back. "I think we'd better begin without them," said Little Bear. "They might be ages."

Bramwell Brown was the first to be judged. He had rolled himself up in a piece of paper and was lying on the floor. "What are you meant to be?" asked Old Bear.

"Bang!" said Bramwell Brown.

"I think it's an exploding sausage," said Little Bear.

"BANG!" said Bramwell Brown even louder.

"I know," said Mo, "it's a Christmas cracker."

"Oh, well done!" said Old Bear. "I can see it is now. What a clever idea!"

King Mo was next. He marched in front of the judges with his cracker crown on and a king's robe made from a piece of red crêpe paper. He looked very smart indeed and everyone cheered.

The next thing to shuffle in front of the judges seemed to be a walking paper chain. It moved along like a brightly colored, rustling snake. "It seems to be a paper chain that can walk," said Little Bear, "but I can't see who's under it."

"It's us, it's us!" cried the little yellow bears, Marigold and Buttercup. "We knew you'd never see us." The paper chain suddenly tripped over its paws and ended up a heap of bears and paper. Marigold and Buttercup grinned at the judges from under the heap. "We're a paper chain that's fallen down now," said Marigold, "they do you know, sometimes."

"Of course they do," said Old Bear, "that's very good."

While everyone was busy clapping for the fallen paper chain, in jumped Rabbit. He was covered in white cotton wool and had a carrot tied over his nose.

"Oh look," cried Little Bear, "a white rabbit."

"I'm not a white rabbit, said Rabbit, crossly, "that wouldn't be Christmasy. "I'm a snowman."

"Well, a snow *rabbit* then," said Little Bear.

"You've left your ears sticking up. Snowmen don't have long ears."

Old Bear fetched a woolly hat and, tucking Rabbit's ears inside it, popped it over the snow-rabbit's head. "There," he said, "you look wonderful now, Rabbit."

While the toys were admiring Rabbit, the door opened and something prickly came in. "What is it?" said King Mo. "It looks like a holly bush." But when they looked closer, the toys could see that inside the bush were two pairs of eyes.

"It's Rosie and Fluff!" said Old Bear. "But what are you supposed to be?"

"We're holly bears," said Rosie, proudly.

"What are holly bears?" asked Rabbit, not sure whether he should know.

"Oh, you know," said Fluff. "There's a Christmas song called 'The Holly and the Ivy' and it's got a bit in it all about holly bears. I don't know what they look like, but they must be something like this." And with that, the whole holly-covered pair of bears did a little twirl to show off its disguise.

"Well, if holly bears look like a bush, then you've done very well," said Old Bear.

When everyone had clapped for the holly bears, Old Bear and Little Bear discussed the winners.

"We really think," said Old Bear "that you've all done so well, you should all win something, but what can the prize be?"

"A crown!" shouted Rosie. "In the Holly Bears' song it says something like, 'the holly bears the crown.' "

"Oh, I remember," said King Mo, "and I know how we can all have a prize *and* a crown."

"How?" asked the others.

"Crackers," said Mo.

On the table in the room had been a whole box of crackers. Mo had only used one to get the crown for his king costume. It had been a box of ten crackers and there were nine left. And so they all won prizes for their costumes and they all felt very much jollier in their paper party hats. There were even enough crackers for the judges to have one each and they did deserve them, didn't they?

SPOTTY BEN

Ben saw his own reflection
In the mirror on the wall.
"I seem to be all spotty;
I can't be well at all."
"It's all right," laughed the other toys,
"None of your spots are new.
You've always had a spotty coat,
That's how we know it's you."

POLLY AND THE WARM SNOWMAN

There had not been a single flake of snow all winter. Almost every morning the toys had crowded eagerly onto the windowsill hoping to look out on to a snow-covered garden. Some of the newer toys had never seen snow and they were just beginning to wonder whether perhaps it didn't really exist.

And then one morning there it was, a thick blanket of snow over everything. They woke up and wondered why it was so quiet. There were no footsteps on the path or wheels on the road, even the birds were too busy keeping warm to sing. The toys almost fell off the windowsill, they were so excited.

"We'll build a snowman," they shouted, and all rushed to the door and tumbled into the garden in a heap.

It was then that they realized just how deep the snow was. Only the tallest teddy bears with the longest legs could actually walk about. Most of the others had disappeared completely. "Oh dear," said the muffled voice of Polly, a particularly small bear, "I can't move at all. The snow is so deep it comes up to my ears."

The others helped to pull her out and then Freddie the teddy fetched a tea tray from the kitchen. All the smaller toys clambered on to the tray and were towed across the snow-covered lawn by the bigger ones. They walked round and round the garden until they found a place that looked just right for their snowman and then they set to work.

Freddie and the other big bears made a snowball and began to roll it across the garden. As it rolled it picked up more and more snow and left a trail of bare grass behind it just like a wiggly green path. The small bears were very pleased to see this and, leaving their tea-tray sledge, they ran along the green path and helped the big bears push the heavy snowball.

After a while the snowball was large enough to be the body of the snowman.

"We need a head now," said Polly, and began to pat a snowball into shape with her paws. They rolled this one right round the lawn making a big O-shaped path and arrived back at the snowman's body with a snowball big enough to be his head.

"How are we going to get it up on top of the body?" asked Freddie. "Even I can't reach."

But Polly had a plan. "We've got the tea tray," she said. "We'll roll the snowball head on to the tray and pull it up with a rope. It shouldn't be too difficult."

They all rolled the snowman's head on to the tray and threaded a skipping rope through the handles. Then the strongest bears climbed up to the top of the snowman's body with the ends of the rope and pulled. Slowly the tea tray, with the snowball head on it, rose into the air until it was level with the bears.

"It's up! We've done it," shouted Freddie, and he rolled the head neatly into place. The toys down below cheered and jumped up and down with excitement.

"He needs a face," called one little bear. The tea tray was lowered down and some of the toys went off to fetch coal for the snowman's eyes, a carrot for his nose and twigs for his mouth and eyebrows.

Very soon the snowman was smiling down at them with his twiggy mouth and his shining, coal-black eyes. Before Freddie climbed down he took off his own stripy scarf and tied it round the neck of the snowman.

"He looks lovely," said Polly. "We'll keep him for ever and ever and come and play with him every day."

They spent the whole afternoon in the garden – throwing snowballs, making slopes out of snow and sliding down them on the tray. When it began to get dark they said goodnight to the snowman and went indoors to bed.

The next morning the sun was shining brightly and the toys couldn't wait to get outside. But when they opened the door they all stopped and stared. "Somebody's stolen our snowman," cried Freddie. It seemed to be true: the lovely snowman had vanished.

Then Polly noticed something lying on the ground. "But they left behind the carrot nose," she said.

"And the coal eyes," added Freddie. "And my scarf."

And then they realized what had happened to their snowman. He hadn't been stolen – he'd melted. What's more, the snow had almost gone too. There wasn't enough to build another snowman. Feeling very sad, the toys began to play with the

last of the snow. But the sun was quite warm now and even the last of the snow was melting fast.

Polly had an idea and went indoors again. The others could see her sitting by the window, knitting. She looked up and waved every now and again, but she seemed very busy.

By the end of the day the grass was as green as it was in summer. The only snow left was in the shady bit under the tree. The toys gave up trying to make things with the snow and trooped indoors.

"It's nearly spring now," said Freddie to Polly, when he found her sitting by the fire. "I don't think it will snow again this winter, so we won't be able to make another snowman for a whole year."

"No," said Polly, "but I have a surprise for you Freddie," and she pointed to a corner of the room. In soft white wool with black eyes and a carrot-shaped nose stood a little knitted snowman. He was smiling at Freddie and was wearing a knitted hat and scarf just like Freddie's own.

"He's a warm snowman, Freddie. I knitted him myself. The outdoor snowman may have melted, but this one never will."

"We can play with him all year," said Freddie. "Oh Polly, you are clever!" And holding one white arm each they led the little warm snowman out of the room to show all the other toys.

Of course, he never melted. In fact, he's still there to this day.

Mr. Brown And The Baby Bear

Mr. and Mrs. Brown were teddy bears. They lived in a little cupboard in the playroom. They had furnished the cupboard home themselves with things that Mr. Brown had found while out walking. He'd brought back acorns for them to use as cups, and soft feathers that he'd found near the duck pond to stuff cushions with. He'd made mirrors from old milk bottle tops and a broom from twigs that he'd collected. All their tables were made from little boxes.

In fact their cupboard was cluttered with the bits and pieces that he'd collected and one day Mrs. Brown decided that it was full enough. "If you go out today," she said to Mr. Brown, "then you are not to come back with anything. I shall check that your paws are empty when you walk in that door."

 Mr. Brown hugged her as usual and set off out of the cupboard, across the room, down the stairs and out into the garden.

It was a lovely autumn day and a

carpet of leaves covered the lawn. Mr. Brown thought it was great fun crunching through the leaves. He found some especially interesting ones which he thought of taking home but, remembering Mrs. Brown's warning, he left them where they were. "It's a pity," he said. "I'm sure I could have made something with them."

A little further down the garden he found a bright, shiny brown chestnut. "Oh, what a beauty!" he said to himself as he bent down to polish the gleaming nut with his paw. "The case it came out of must have been huge." And then he saw it – the biggest, most perfect chestnut shell he'd ever seen. The inside was silken smooth and white and shaped like a round-bottomed bowl. The outside was hard and covered in prickles.

"I'm sure I could put something in it," said Mr. Brown, but he remembered Mrs. Brown and sadly left it where it was.

Mr. Brown continued down the garden until he came to the fence at the end. He was just about to turn and go back to the house when he saw a heap of leaves. They had been raked up the day before and piled against the fence.

Mr. Brown gazed at the heap and sighed.

There was one thing he'd always wanted to do and that was to jump right into the middle of

a heap of dry, crunchy autumn leaves.

Shall I, he thought to himself. Just to see what it's like – to see whether it's soft or crunchy or bouncy. I must find out.

And, looking round to make sure nobody was watching, he climbed up on the fence above the leaves.

"One, two, three," he said out loud – and then he jumped. It was wonderful. The leaves were all crispy and they crackled softly as he sank gently down, down, down, into the springy heap.

And then, when he'd stopped sinking into the leaves, Mr. Brown heard a sound. Someone, or something, very near him said, "Ow!"

"Well, that wasn't me," said Mr. Brown. "I'm not hurt."

"Well, I am," said a little muffled voice. "You're sitting on me."

Mr. Brown jumped to his feet and, pushing his paw deep into the leaves, he pulled out the smallest teddy bear you've ever seen.

"Goodness!" said Mr. Brown. "It's Toby Small. How did you get in there?"

"Somebody took me for a walk and dropped me," said Toby Small, "and then I was raked up with the leaves. I've been here all night and I'm cold and hungry."

"Well, Toby," said Mr. Brown, "I shall take you back to your house this afternoon, but first I think I'd better take you home to Mrs. Brown so you can have the leaves brushed out of your fur."

So Mr. Brown picked up the little bear and carried him back to the house. On the way, he stopped to collect the big chestnut shell that he'd found. He had an idea now how he could use it without making Mrs. Brown cross.

Mrs. Brown was waiting at the door of the cupboard when he arrived back.

"Now," she said to Mr. Brown when she saw the chestnut shell in his paws, "take that straight back to the garden. We don't need it."

"But we do," said Mr. Brown, and he put down the chestnut shell so that Mrs. Brown could see inside it. There, lying fast alseep in the soft, smooth, white bed was Toby Small. He was tucked up with sheets made from the brightest autumn leaves and he was smiling happily.

"Oh," said Mrs. Brown softly, "I see. You couldn't really leave him outside, could you?" And she carried the sleeping bear in his chestnut cot into the little cupboard house.

When Toby Small had had a sleep and a meal and his fur was brushed free of leaves, Mr. and Mrs. Brown took him home. And after that he

came to stay with them for his holidays and they kept the chestnut shell for him to sleep in.

Gradually the cupboard house became more and more cluttered with things that Mr. Brown brought home from his walks, but Mrs. Brown never complained. "We must have something for Toby Small to play with when he comes to stay," she would say. And Mr. Brown just smiled.

HAZEL'S NIGHT OUT

Hazel the little brown donkey and Edward Bear were the very best of friends. They went everywhere and played everything together. Sometimes Hazel pulled Edward round in a little cart and sometimes Edward would pull the cart and give Hazel a ride just for a change. At night when they were tired they tucked themselves into a little corner of the windowsill behind the curtain. Hazel liked to gaze out of the window and dream that she was sleeping in a field like a real donkey. Edward would tuck the curtain round him, snuggle up to Hazel and dream that he was exactly where he really was, in a nice cosy corner of the playroom with his very best friend.

"Why do you pretend you're outside?" Edward asked Hazel one day. "You'd be cold and miserable if you really slept in a field."

"Of course I wouldn't," said the little donkey. "I have thick fur to keep me warm."

"Well, I'm quite happy to stay inside," said Edward.

They settled down in their usual place that

night, but next morning when Edward woke up, Hazel was nowhere to be seen. Edward sat down to try and remember where he'd last seen his friend. "Now," he said to himself, "was she definitely with me last night?" But he already knew the answer. "Yes, of course she was, because she was talking about how nice it would be to sleep in a field." Then, "Oh no," he said out loud, "perhaps Hazel has gone outside."

Edward rushed to look out of the window. It was pouring with rain. The grass glistened, the trees dripped and the sky looked as grey as old saucepans. Edward looked at the lawn and he looked at the hedge, and then he looked at the field beyond the hedge, and then he saw Hazel. She was standing quite still in the middle of the field staring at the ground.

"She's there!" cried Edward, "she's outside in the field. I'm going out to get her."

Lots of the other toys said they would come too and soon a crowd of them, wrapped in coats and under umbrellas was trudging across the lawn.

"Hazel," called Edward, "come in! You'll get soaked."

"I can't," called Hazel.

"What does she mean, she can't?" said one of the other toys.

"I don't know," said Edward. "I'll go and find out."

Edward made his way across the field until he came to his old friend. "Hazel," he said, "have you been out here all night?"

"Yes," said Hazel, sadly.

"And are you coming in now?"

"No," said Hazel.

"Why not?" asked Edward.

"Because I'm so wet that my legs are all heavy with rain and I can't walk," said Hazel, miserably.

"Oh, I see," said Edward, and patted his friend gently. Sure enough Hazel's fur was so full of rain water that she felt like a sponge. "Can't you walk at all?" asked Edward.

"Not at all," said Hazel. "My hooves feel as though they are fixed to the ground."

"Don't worry," said Edward, "I think I may have the answer."

Rushing back to the house, he fetched the little cart that Hazel usually pulled. Then, with some of the other toys, he dragged it across the field to the soggy donkey. With everyone pushing and pulling

75

they heaved Hazel into the back of the cart and trundled her across the field and back to the house. Once inside they tipped her out and everyone set to work to rub her fur dry. At last the poor donkey could move again.

"Real donkeys don't get wet, do they?" said Hazel.

"Not as wet as you," said Edward, kindly. "But you're not a real donkey, you're a toy donkey and toys have to stay dry."

But to make his friend feel more like a real donkey, Edward cut out a picture of a shiny star and pinned it to the curtain. "Now you can look up and pretend you're outside," he said, kindly. "This way you can sleep under the stars and stay dry."

"I like that," said Hazel, gazing at the star. "I think I shall be happy to sleep indoors now."